The Red Branch Review

No. 1

Editorial Board

Table of Contents

My Brother Has Ten Years
by Ashley Massey

My brother has ten years
to feel the concrete walls
hug his tall, lean body, scarred
from the possessed scratches
of pharmaceutical profits.

My brother has ten years
to hear a CO kill his name
and leave a number in its grave.

My brother has ten years
to walk with his eyes
glued to the back of his head,
watching for a quick flash of metal.

My brother has ten years
to sit and think about his first love
and how his pill-filled palm
opened up her death door.

My brother has ten years
to protest to a parole board
that believes him
like Thomas believed Jesus.

My brother has ten years
to wash away his sins
in the laundry of a stranger
for thirty cents an hour.

My brother has ten years
to write letters to the dead
that he doesn't need a stamp for.

My brother has ten years
to watch his son grow up
through glass and red eyes.

My brother has ten years
to ask for commissary,
but our pockets are already turned out,
empty from demons who
twist laws into tricks.

My brother has ten years
to stare at the phone
on the concrete wall
after I stop answering.

The Saddest Song

had black hair
we sang it once
despair choking my heart
driving home

the fried chicken sign
singing gypsy sweetheart.

John Dorsey

Not in the Cards
by Ace Boggess

I could beat the weatherman at poker,
sitting across a table
while he nervously laughs at his awful jokes
then calls when he should fold.
He's wrong more often than accurate,
his every breath a bluff, bluster,
missing the percentages.
Snow, he said last week, & rain fell hard.
Ice storm, he said, *hazardous*.
The sun shone throughout a day.
The weatherman misreads his hands,
raises on sailboats into a possible flush.
I've learned the tells of his eyes
that lack a chill of stillness.
Blizzard, he says as if claiming aces
when he has seven-deuce off-suited.
Outside, winter is a paradise
with empty streets of gold.

An Interview with Frank X Walker

A native of Danville Kentucky and a former Kentucky Poet Laureate, Frank X Walker is a professor in the department of English and the African American and Africana Studies Program at the University of Kentucky and the founding editor of *Pluck! The Journal of Affrilachian Arts & Culture*. A Cave Canem Fellow and co-founder of the Affrilachian Poets, he is the author of eight collections of poetry including, *Turn Me Loose: The Unghosting of Medgar Evers*, winner of the 2014 NAACP Image Award for Outstanding Poetry; and *Buffalo Dance: The Journey of York*, winner of the Lillian Smith Book Award as well as two newer collections, *The Affrilachian Sonnets* and *About Flight*.

X, his preferred moniker, has dedicated much of his career to upsetting the poetic and cultural status-quo and prying open the national consciousness as it relates to notions of Appalachia. He coined the term Affrilachia and is dedicated to deconstructing and forcing a new definition of what it means to be Appalachian. He is a Lannan Poetry Fellowship Award recipient has degrees from the University of Kentucky and Spalding University as well as three honorary doctorates from the University of Kentucky, Spalding University and Transylvania University.

X has accomplished his work not just through poetry, but through service, as founder/Executive Director of the Bluegrass Black Arts Consortium, the Program Coordinator of the University of Kentucky's King Cultural Center, and the Assistant Director of Purdue University's Black Cultural Center. He has held board positions for the Kentucky Humanities Council, Appalshop and the Kentucky Writers Coalition as well as a government appointment to Cabinet for Education, Arts & Humanities and the Committee on Gifted Education. He has served as vice president of the Kentucky Center for the Arts and the executive director of Kentucky's Governor's School for the Arts.

The following conversation was conducted electronically over the Summer of 2021 and has been lightly edited for clarity.

Noah Soltau, Managing Editor

INTERVIEWER
As a poet, you clearly believe in the power of the word. With that in mind, talk to me about the idea of Affrilachian poetry and literature.

The word stopped traffic and created an opportunity for new literature and ideas to enter regional conversations and classrooms. It is essential that the new conversations happening embrace the historical data that clearly illustrates that diversity in this region is not a new truth, but an inconvenient casualty in the well-monied effort to advance an idea of a too-easily caricatured "throw away" space, ripe for exploitation by corporate interests. The environmental and human casualties continue to go unmentioned in the national conversation. Poetry and literature is but one way to draw more attention to these truths.

INTERVIEWER

You stand at the gates of several powerful institutions, as a professor and prominent literary voice. How do you use that power for good, and what advice do you have for younger poets who find themselves in positions of cultural or institutional authority?

X

I don't see my position as one of power. I do acknowledge the potential influence I might have on readers and students alike. To that end, I just focus on truth and the responsibility to tell it with a focus on marginalized, muted, or silenced voices. And I urge them to consider the same.

INTERVIEWER

Language and identity are intimately and inextricably intertwined in your work. In "Talking in Tongues," you explore the different ways your mother would speak, and to whom. How did the realizations that there were different ways of using and even embodying language and where and when those were safe to use influence your poetic voice?

X

Somewhere between my first kiss and my first heartbreak, I discovered that poetry had even more power when used in the service of others. Everything I learned about language growing up at my mother's skirt influenced what I understood about communication which ultimately shaped my poetic voice.

INTERVIEWER

You carry the notion of the relationship between family and language powerfully forward in "Last Will, Last Testament." Constance Alexander noted that the collection frames you, the poet, as a conduit between past and future. If a person "is not dead until the people no longer speak their names," what sort of life-giving or life-affirming power does the poem, the written and spoken word, have?

X

I don't know that poetry can create or give life, but it certainly can help let readers and listeners know that they are most certainly alive. Every time a poem moves you in any direction, emotionally it is doing that necessary work.

INTERVIEWER

To change the focus from the heavy social and political weight that your poetry often bears, what feels the best about creating poetry, from what do you derive the greatest aesthetic pleasure?

X

I don't know the answer to this question, but I am always pleased at what happens at live readings, when it's clear that the attempt at communicating was successful. I admit that I experience a different kind of satisfaction when I think a new poem is finished, but nothing like the satisfaction of opening a brand new book for the first time.

INTERVIEWER

Tell me a little bit about how you grew into your poetic voice.

X

I think I'm still growing into my voice. Because I think of myself as a failed fiction writer who uses poetry to sharpen his skills, and because I write so often in other people's voices, I haven't spent a lot of time thinking about my own voice. Whatever comfort zone I currently enjoy regarding having a poetic voice is simply the product of putting in the work in the classroom and on the page, including reading and discussing the work, for the proverbial "10,000 hours" it allegedly takes to become competent at anything.

INTERVIEWER

What are you most excited about when you look at the current group of Affrilachian poets?

X

I'm most excited about their potential. You can literally hear the books inthem when they talk about their work.

INTERVIEWER

What would you like to tell yourself, back in 1991 at that "Best of Appalachian Writing" meeting that served as the springboard for the Affrilachian movement, that would have offered you some assurance that you were doing something important and worthwhile?

X

Nothing. I think that kind of pressure would have sabotaged my creativity and my work ethic. I didn't need assurance that what I was doing was important and worthwhile. It felt natural and it felt good and it put me in conversation with a group of others that have become lifelong friends. That was assurance enough.

Sushi for Hillbillies
by Susan O'Dell Underwood

It's posh in East Tennessee tonight.

Thursday maki rolls are half-price
and all-American—tempura deep-fried
with cream cheese, smoked trout, and sauce that's nothing
if not mayonnaise's kissing cousin.

In line for the ladies room, these two are Pentecostal,
one with untrimmed lank and holy hair,
the other with a braid hanging nearly to the hem
of her acid-washed blue jean skirt.
She's preaching over again what she preached
to some poor man who's lost and bound for certain.
"I told him, if you sin, you're going to hell.
There's nothing to it besides that."

It's a thin vein of roe that calls us home,
reminds us of the small-mouth bass we split open
long ago on some rickety back porch table,
in view of the cow field and the river
rising up into fog against the mountains.

Now we dine on precious flesh we must practice
to pronounce: *maguro, ikura, unagi, nori,*
daikon some local boy juliennes
to earn eight bucks an hour.

This is the extravagance that tempted me
when I used to make-believe grown-up,
wishing my parents owned martini glasses,
praying someday I'd cross over
to that other, blissful side, sophisticated and redeemed.
Now we've all arrived, our coveting accomplished.
We're proud our Southern portions are on equal terms
with tender bites they pinch in chopsticks
from Santa Barbara to Boston.

But we're like koi, those giant gold fish transformed,
our copper scales grown crimson, larger
and outgrowing, bound forever round and round,
a swelling fatuous luxury
of being bigger than the day before,
in those same backwaters where
we were bred, still circling.

Proselyte
by Greg Ramkawsky

Sun visor cluttered with the paraphernalia
Devout shrine for daily worship

Sacred heart of Jesus shining
From the chest of a white man

With shoulder-length brown hair
And a beard, two fingers extended

As if to say, "Yep, I'm the man...God
...God-man..." as if to demonstrate some

Pronounced blessing, his fixed gaze
Leading to the Blesséd virgin

Her alabaster glance aimed
At preventing the culmination of lust

And loneliness, her image partially covering
The Powerball tickets that missed

And the scratch-offs that are worth
The cost of more scratch-offs when

They're turned in at the local gas station
Worth a roll of Redman or

Wintergreen Kodiak and a case of
Keystone Light, the dented empties

Rolling in the bed like convictions
Saint Christopher holding the clutter

With a spring clip – flip the visor down
During sunset, traveling back to the singlewide

In memoriam, in loving memory,
 "I will always watch over thee"

Partially stained by coffee when
The funeral card fell to the vinyl floor

And laid for two weeks before
Being tucked away next to the mirror

With the spider crack revealing
The flaws in the face, squinting

As the way to the road home tunneled
Then lengthened, the sun shining

The fingers of light gesturing Through
the dappled tree shade.

The Pond
by Elaine Fowler Palencia

The pond lies in a pasture
near the red dirt road
that borders its small farm.
Just now, thirst slaked,
its cows have withdrawn
to the shade of distant trees.
The pond dreams under its slicker
of sunlight as a dragonfly
stitches through its cattails.
It listens to the talk
of passing sow bugs, ants,
spiders, dung beetles,
butterflies, mosquitoes.
It mirrors the glide
of a redwing blackbird
and exclaims as a bullfrog
fleeing the Tennessee heat
plops into its shallows,
sending its minnows darting.

Fifty years ago
my grandfather died
and the farm was sold
to a corporation
that made rayon.
To build their plant,
they leveled
the pastures, road, and woods
and filled in the pond.
In time the rayon outfit
sold out to a company
that makes fiberglass. Now
there are whispers
of asbestos contamination.

No one remembers
that there once was a pond,
blinking in the rough grass
like a blue eye of sky.
Here: let it abide with you.

Blue Mornings
by Peter Faziani

Michael woke to five notifications from his mother. During the night his aunt, a woman he had not seen much since seeing altogether too much of her, stumbling in as she stood naked changing on her second wedding day, had succumbed to Alzheimer's. He had been a twelve-year-old boy, and the wedding was in his house, and he was just going about his summer. His mother and Abigail weren't twins, but out of five children they were the closest.

Abigail passed twenty minutes ago.
Evelyn and I were able to say goodbye.

I love you, Mike.

Abigail was sitting in her lounge chair awake and conscious the entire time. She wasn't talking, Her face looked so calm. No wrinkles.

Every other time I saw her I would think and hope she'd jump up and say 'oh just kidding, you guys. I'm ok.' But not tonight.

I'm glad I had Evelyn there.

Saturday, when Friday night's liquor had worn off, he called his mother back from bed, but it went to voicemail. After hanging up, he realized that his message was awkward, "Hey…uh…I just woke up…I know what you went through must've been difficult, but it was best for Abigail. Call me back when you wake up… if you need to talk. Love you."

Michael got out of bed. His family had been awake for at least an hour. Already watching tv in the living room. He staged his expression walking down the stairs as he heard the girls laughing at the childish tone coming from their cartoons.

"Daddy!"

"Good morning, Panda," Mike muttered. He couldn't help but feel buoyed as she lit up. "How long have you been awake? He asked but quickly added, "Why didn't someone come get me?"

"We tried. You just grumbled and covered your head with the blanket," Adaline said.

"My name's not Panda! It's A Yay," his three-year-old daughter, AJ, replied.

"Aa Yay. Got it," he said as he sat down between the kids on the couch. He saw a cup of coffee steaming in his wife's hands and asked, "Did you make an entire pot?"

"Yes? " she wrinkled her eyebrows and cocked her head to the side.

"Great," he said as he walked into the kitchen and pulled a mug imprinted with two Disney princesses on it down from the cupboard.

Michael heard Marcie hesitate for a minute in the living room. She must have been listening to him calm his breathing as he filled the mug. She must have heard him put the carafe back onto the hotplate.

"You okay?" Marcie asked when she finally followed him into the kitchen. He saw her eyes dart to the empty bourbon bottle on the counter.

Mike waited until she stood before him, puzzled. "Alzheimer's finally took Abigail." He didn't know what to say next exactly. "I haven't talked to my mom yet. She texted me last night. She was on her way home with Evelyn."

"I'm sorry," Marcie said quietly. She didn't seem surprised.

"Well," Michael said, because he wasn't surprised either, not really. "I know she's been planning this for a while."

This they considered, and then, though they both said nothing, had the same thought: how do you explain this to your children?

The coffee did not burn his tongue, another affirmation that everyone but Michael had been up for a while. He took a drink and let his eyes turn toward the floor. Death was one thing. This was something more.

He had killed the conversation.

In the living room, *Bluey* rang out over the tv.

"Daddy," AJ shouted, "come sit with us."

"Okay," Michael said and walked back into the living room because what else?

The Walnut Street Bridge
Reflections on Monday, March 19, 1906
by John C. Mannone

It was on the cusp of spring, like now, when I painted this 1890 bridge. I stood on the southern shore of the Tennessee, and my canvas caught the filtered light through the nimbus clouds. The river snaked through the lush forest-garden, through the heart of Chattanooga. The Tennessee is true to its name, *Tanasi*—the place where the river bends, where the green water meets itself, where the pastoral terrain is full of peace. But do not be deceived. I stared at the colored bridge—once bright blue, now softened under the withering sun—arched over the Moccasin Bend water, its rye brown murk streaking through algae; sloshing the stained limestone pillars. On that day, the river seemed to cry, its elegiac tone rippling the water. I sensed the urgency of the river flow—as if it were carrying secrets far away—driven by undercurrents and a hapless wind, perhaps to assuage a certain kind of guilt when all creation groans.

The view of the second span in its Camelback truss design was particularly beautiful and ugly, indifferent and poignant. I held my breath to arrest the quiver in my hands, but the pigments at the end of my brush must have sensed I was still troubled. In the crux of the girders, their steel shadows failed to conceal all of it. Nor the rust—color of dried blood—could hide the ligature on the beams themselves from the sway and fray of rope that once hung there with a young Black man dangling on its end. Just like before. My canvas couldn't quite capture the right shade in those innocent flecks of red, the spilled blood. I heard the whispers in the latticework of the bridge: echoes from the crack of fifty some bullets that riddled his body, its thump after falling on the bridge walk when a bullet severed the hemp, the shattering of his skull from yet another five shots—point blank to the head, the raucous jeers from the crowd, the caws of crows drowning out his words of forgiveness for his murderers.

History cannot hide the bullet holes any more than the bridge's wooden walkway could. Still life. And there's always a bigger problem. I could not find the depth of blackness in the corners of the beams, or in the swirls of water in the deepening umbra of the waves, nor could I understand the grave color and texture of human hatred.

On March 19, 1906, Chattanooga, Tennessee, Ed Johnson was hanged from the second span of the Walnut Street Bridge, and brutally mutilated for allegedly attacking and raping a white woman. Years later he was proven innocent.

Winner of the 2017 Joy Margrave Award (curated by Tennessee Mountain Writers)

A Note From the Visual Arts Editor on the Work of Kelly Hider and Alice Stone-Collins

The work of these two artists invites a voyeuristic reading: one peering into the intimate spaces and sinister banality of suburban life, the other borrowing the family photos of unknown subjects leaving gaps in context that make it difficult not to stare through the holes in curiosity and wonder. Through ambiguity, humor, and sumptuous beauty they draw in the viewer, implicating them in the process. With her altered found imagery, Hider goes beyond Kodachrome nostalgia, presenting a past haunted by the missing and obscured by shimmering glitter. Her works call into question the authenticity of the photographic image, while remaining deeply intent on the power those same images hold. Through painted collages, Stone-Collins explores the slow buildup of the mundane paraphernalia of life, subversive toys, and unsettling suburban landscapes. In her works, these elements are layered in dramatic and witty scenes sometimes referencing grand altarpieces, sometimes modest shrines, all in tribute to the personal relationships and historical traumas that shape us. Both these artists question if we are coming or going, if we are lost or found, and if the concept of returning home is real or simply imagined. I hope you enjoy the journey with each of them as much as I did.

An Interview with Kelly Hider

Through photo-editing and surface manipulations, Kelly Hider's work traces threads within an existing domestic visual narrative, as well as creating new ones. The carefully applied surface embellishments suggest human care, and by altering these found images and presenting them in a gallery setting, they are given new life and purpose. Photoshop tools are used to highlight both the presence and absence of subject, and an exposed vulnerability to the passage of time. The surface glitter embellishments are both seductive and unsettling. She uses a variety of vernacular photographic source material – Kodachrome slides from the 1950s, antique black and white photos from the 1930s, and family snapshots from the 1980s. Existing first as an object, then scanned and digitized, and enlarged and printed, from these images many stories emerge: some personal, some universal, others surreal and fictitious.

Kelly Hider is a regionally and nationally exhibiting studio artist living in Knoxville, Tennessee. She received her BFA from SUNY Brockport in 2007, and an MFA from the University of Tennessee in 2011. Recent solo shows include exhibits at Unrequited Leisure in Nashville, the Central Collective in Knoxville, the Clayton Arts Center in Maryville, TN, and Lincoln Memorial University. Hider's work was featured on the cover of the independent art journal, *Number: Inc.* in 2016, and she has been twice awarded Ann & Steve Bailey Opportunity Grants through the Arts & Culture Alliance's Heritage Fund in Knoxville. A proud Hambidge Fellow, Hider completed an artist residency at the Hambidge Center in Rabun Gap, Georgia in 2019. Kelly Hider works at Arrowmont School of Arts and Crafts as their Youth Education Programs Manager, facilitating Arrowmont's local programming and outreach for area kids and young adults, as well as the new youth outreach program, *ArtReach on the Road*, which brings craft education to K-12 students throughout central Appalachia. Hider recently joined the Tennessee Craft Board in 2021.

The following interview was conducted electronically over the summer of 2022. It has been edited for length and clarity.

Heather Hartman, Visual Arts Editor

INTERVIEWER

We should probably start with your use of found imagery, since it's so integral to your work. What meaning does the found image hold for you?

HIDER

I've always been interested in the false "truth" that photos hold. How people often feel like photos tell the truth and capture something real, but there's so much that's inferred and invented when it's just a single image without context. And found images always exist in this space without context of what came before or after the photo was taken, or who was taking the photo and why—and the viewer naturally fills in that information with their own experience. And that's what I do when I'm sorting through found images, projecting my own experience and feelings and narrative onto it.

INTERVIEWER

Yes, they definitely seem very personal in that way. I think some people would initially read the use of these types of images as nostalgic, but your work feels more like it's addressing the haunting of a space and time rather than the longing for something past. Can you talk about those haunting presences? What is absent that also creates a sense of the image being haunted?

HIDER

I'm glad you can feel that when looking at my work. Sometimes people are nostalgic for the past, but others are haunted by the past; I feel like I find myself on that side of it most of the time. I'm drawn to images where I can insert my own slightly unsettling or fantastical feeling or story into the image, either with digital manipulation or the surface embellishments. Or, like you said, by eliminating subject from the image to create an absence, or conversely inserting a presence into a piece to create that haunted feeling.

I'm also always interested in one of the fundamental concepts of photography: that by capturing the fleeting moment, photos are also capturing and preserving the death of a moment, and that somehow photos embody that idea of death. Especially older, found photos that are objects you can hold (as opposed to digital images,) the photo object sort of becomes a reliquary.

INTERVIEWER

Oh, that's so interesting! Do you think at all about the physical appearance of reliquaries in relation to your work?

HIDER

I haven't, but I do think about my work relating to the gold-leaf accents found in historic paintings and mosaics from the Byzantine and proto-Renaissance periods.

I know collage was very important to you in your early work when you were making slightly more traditional paintings. Do you still think of your work in relation to collage?

HIDER
Yes, collage is a big part of my early work, and even when I painted, I'd often collage xerox copies of images into the paintings or incorporate xerox transfers. It was a slow transition to where the painting components became less and less, and the found image took over, becoming the entire surface to jump off of.

I suppose one way that collage is still present in the work is with regard to the repetition of imagery. I often will use just a handful of photos when composing a body of work or exhibit and make several pieces using the same image, although the digital or glitter manipulations will vary within each piece. Sometimes I just have more to explore or say with that image, but it's also a way to tie the pieces together and create a visual echo when they're all together in a gallery space.

INTERVIEWER
And the glitter! Why does the use of glitter appeal to you, especially considering your training as a painter?

HIDER
I've always been interested in alternative materials and their implications. The craft store glitter, (and in the past, plastic craft rhinestones,) interest me as a material, firstly because they're sparkly—who doesn't love sparkles and glitter? But also because I like that my work creates a high art/low art conversation. I buy this glitter at Joann fabrics or online. Martha Stewart has a fine glitter line, ha! These are not real rhinestones and diamond dust; they're cheap imitations. Also most people understand glitter and how to use it (you lay down glue, shake out the glitter over it, and let it dry), and that accessibility is important to me. Painting, on the other hand, can be an inaccessible form of art to a lot of people. It's unfortunate but true that modern painting through to the present comes off as pretentious or obtuse, and can be alienating. By incorporating everyday found objects like clocks, fabric, umbrellas, cardboard, or detritus, Robert Rauschenberg was trying to break down that barrier. He was trying to both elevate the importance of everyday life, and temper that high-art inaccessibility. I try to do the same thing, to be welcoming to all viewers by my material choices: everyday family photographs and craft store materials.

INTERVIEWER
Your work is heavily digital and uses so much borrowed imagery, yet still feels like there is a real sense of your touch that is consistent throughout

these pieces. How do you think about your artist's hand? Do you have any other historical references that help frame your sense of touch in the work?

HIDER
That's a great question that I think about all of the time. Having been trained in painting and drawing, I hold dear the importance of mark-making and the artist's hand. It's important to me that the artist's touch is present, and that there is a "wow" moment when the viewer looks at the glitter embellishments; some of them are very intricate. I mix all of the glitter I use to match the colors underneath in the photograph, not unlike mixing paint, and have a huge shelf in my studio of jars of mixed glitter colors. It can be labor intensive when I'm working on an intricate section of a piece with multiple colors, both to "draw" with the glue and a tiny paintbrush, but also that I have to wait 24 hours for one color to dry before I can brush off the glitter and lay down another color next to it. I think about Botticelli's paintings a lot when I'm making these intricate glitter sections, and the very, very thin strands of gold leaf that were added to the surface of those paintings to highlight individual strands of the women's hair.

INTERVIEWER
I think the fantastical sensibility in your work is really evident in the landscapes. Can you talk about the way you manipulate color in *Content Aware* or *Meadow* for example?

HIDER
In those two pieces, and the other in-color pieces featured, the color actually wasn't manipulated at all! These pieces are created using Kodachrome slides from the 1950s and 60s, and that type of film just inherently has this hyper-color that I just love! That very first reason I was drawn to this collection of images was because of that intense, surreal hyper-color of the images.

In the *Neon Glow* pieces (*Trillium, Family Portrait,* and *Patricia,*) that hyper-color was stripped away using a Photoshop filter called "Neon Glow." I liked two things about it. One is that, in fine art, using those Photoshop filters is so taboo. It was fun to lean into one as a way to nod to the digital part of my process. And two, I also just really love the feel of this filter as compared to the colorful pieces. Stripped of that color, they feel exposed, or look a little like an x-ray, even. For me, it makes the pieces feel really vulnerable.

INTERVIEWER
Yeah! I read them as faded or ghostly, like they are in danger of disappearing altogether. Is that a consideration for you? Do you feel like you are resurrecting or preserving these images that might otherwise be lost?

HIDER

Oh, of course! I do feel like I'm resurrecting these images, not only from being lost and overlooked, but elevating their status and importance. These images make their way from an object in someone's personal family collection, which is a fairly private and personal space, to being enlarged and presented in a gallery setting.

INTERVIEWER

So how do you decide which images to use?

HIDER

That's one of my favorite parts of my studio practice: combing through photographs. Sometimes I'm sifting through a box of photographs at an antique store, or sometimes it's old photos people are selling on Etsy, or a personal family collection. The photos that jump out at me are the ones where I can see room for manipulation, ones where I can insert myself or insert something new to guide the photo's narrative. That's exciting to me: to find an image that the original, anonymous photographer, myself, and the viewer can all collaborate to give the image new meaning.

Visual Art:
Kelly Hider

Kelly Hider, *The Artist 1,*
Digitized Kodachrome slide, Photoshop, inkjet print, glitter flocking
24"x 18", 2019

Kelly Hider, *Trillium*
Digitized Kodachrome slide, Photoshop, inkjet print, glitter flocking
14″ x 9.75″, 2019

Kelly Hider *Content Aware*
Digitized Kodachrome slide, Photoshop, inkjet print, glitter flocking
25" x 24", 2019

Kelly Hider *Neon Glow (Trillium)*
Digitized Kodachrome slide, Photoshop, inkjet print, glitter flocking
33" x 24", 2019

Kelly Hider *Twilight,*
Digitized Kodachrome slide, Photoshop, inkjet print, glitter flocking
12″ x 8.5″, 2019

Kelly Hider *Neon Glow (Patricia)*
Digitized Kodachrome slide, Photoshop, inkjet print, glitter flocking
12" x 8.5", 2019

Kelly Hider, *Meadow*, Digitized Kodachrome slide, Photoshop, inkjet print, glitter flocking
24" x 28, , 2019

Kelly Hider, *Selection 2 (Family Portrait)*, Digitized Kodachrome slide, Photoshop, inkjet print, glitter flocking
24″ x 36″, 2019

Kelly Hider, *Offering,*
Digitized Kodachrome slide, Photoshop, inkjet print, glitter flocking
4"x 3.5"x 3.5", 2019

Kelly Hider, *Neon Glow (Family Portrait)*, Digitized Kodachrome slide, Photoshop, inkjet print, glitter flocking
16″ x 24″, 2019

Kelly Hider, *The Artist 2*,
Digitized Kodachrome slide, Photoshop, inkjet print, glitter flocking
24"x 18", 2019

An Interview with Alice Stone-Collins

As a child growing up in the woods of northeast Georgia, Alice Stone-Collins chased fireflies at night and traded friendship bracelets by day. While she has lived and worked in the Midwest and the mountains of Colorado, the spaces of her upbringing have continued to haunt and track through her work. Asking questions of tradition and resistant to the ties that bind, her work questions if beauty can come from the mundane, the everyday, the apparent dead. Alice earned her MFA in studio art from the University of Tennessee and has exhibited her work regionally and nationally. She has been a resident artist at KMAC (Kentucky Museum of Art and Craft) based out of Louisville, Kentucky and the David and Julia White Artist Colony in Ciudad Colon, Costa Rica. Alice has been featured on *Studio Break* and *The Artists Mother Podcast* and her work published as the cover art for *Aurora*, The Allegory Ridge Poetry Anthology. She was also a finalist for the Jean-Claude Reynal Scholarship among other honors and awards. Currently, Alice is a faculty member at Georgia Gwinnett College in Metro Atlanta, where she invites others to explore and expose smaller and larger worlds of possibility.

She contends that we are constantly coming home and leaving. We lose; we add; we change. There is a commonness and uniqueness to these experiences. Stale spaces—the mall parking lot, an empty community pool, a neighborhood cul-de-sac at dawn—are subjects that come alive by exploring their contrasting energies of boredom and beauty, stasis and comfort. Places close to home yet tinged with certain mythic qualities of wondering how you arrived here. These are the places her eyes have always been drawn to. Through intricate hand-painted collages, she tries to capture what is arriving and what is taking flight.

This interview was conducted electronically over the summer of 2022, and has been edited for brevity and clarity with permission from the artist.

Heather Hartman, Visual Arts Editor

INTERVIEWER

Some of your work is set in these very banal, suburban and domestic spaces, yet there's this sense of something sinister or maybe even apocalyptic about these scenes. Can you talk about that?

STONE-COLLINS

Yeah, definitely. I don't know if I ever thought of them as apocalyptic but, yeah, I'll take that! When we lived in Indiana and even in Boulder, we were not living in a kind of a typical subdivision with an HOA. But when we moved back to Atlanta that was basically all we had to choose from based on where we worked and where our kids were going to go to school.

Unfortunately, we had to think about all that. I'd love to live downtown but that just wasn't really an option. So that's how we ended up in the suburbs. I just remember kind of like being amazed going to my first HOA meeting. I think we spent like 30 minutes talking about the type of grass that people planted in their yard and just being like, "Okay, this is where I am now."

During that time, we moved back because my mom was sick and I needed to help out with her and my husband wasn't super happy in his previous job, but it had been a long time since we had lived back in Georgia. My husband got really depressed, and he went through a lot of mental health issues. I think viewing the world while going through that and also living in these picture-perfect houses where people are concerned about their picture-perfect lives and how it appeared on the outside—it really just made me kind of become more introspective about these little plots of land with these houses. I can look a couple houses down and see one that looks just like mine but it's a different color.

Then I started to do some research about suburbs in general and about how most of them were created out of segregation, and you know, white flight. So I was thinking about that and having to process and digest those ideas on top of already being back in an area that was politically very different than the area I had just come from. I also started thinking about how I'm literally sitting on land that used to belong to the Muscogee and the Cherokee. So I was thinking about all of those things, but also documenting what is right in front of me, because I've always done that. But this became a lot more personal when I was really having to think about my husband's situation and the situation I'm raising my kids in. It was a little more like "Oh this is it. How am I going to talk about this? How are we going to address this?" So yes, mundane scenes but I feel like they're loaded.

INTERVIEWER
Specifically *Over That Rainbow* and *Special Order 120* give me that sense. In those two there is something about the invasive nature of the fire and the kudzu that operate in the same way.

STONE-COLLINS
Yeah, so Special Order 120 was the set of orders in the Civil War to go burn Atlanta and when we moved here in 2016, it was that next year I think, so 2017, I-85 caught on fire. It was partially because I think there were unhoused people living under the interstate, but mainly the Georgia Department of Transportation had also just kind of neglected it and left all these very flammable substances under the bridge. I just remember watching it on the news, and again thinking about piecing together the past and the present, and just trying to make amends and become okay with it. Again I think a lot of what was bothering my husband at the time were questions of why'd we move back here, why are we subjecting our kids to this Southern mentality. At that time Trump had just been elected

so it was very much like... well, you felt like the world was ending just a little bit and so it seemed very appropriate. It was a couple of years before I made that piece, but that interstate fire really stayed with me. I really tried to think back about how I could connect it to other issues in the past, history coming full-circle.

INTERVIEWER

That brings me to the idea of the landscape or the setting in your work being a stage where some sort of drama can occur, sometimes in humorous ways. I know you're working with collage, so I wondered if you think of them that way, as stages or characters?

STONE-COLLINS

Yeah, when I describe my work to people I actually describe them as felt boards, you know when you were growing up as a kid and you had those felt boards and you could make different scenes? Also, I loved playing with doll houses as a kid, but I didn't really play with them. I just liked setting up the scenes and then I would walk away. That was what I enjoyed about all those things: felt boards, sticker books, and so I think that same kind of concept comes into my method of how I collage. I am definitely thinking about creating these little vignettes, or altarpieces, or almost like creating little memorials. Then also I'm thinking about collage with the different layers of a piece. So just like you were saying, sometimes they are kind of funny, sometimes sinister, sometimes it just looks like a collection of our lives, or a neighborhood scene.

For example, in the refrigerator piece, I was really thinking about an altarpiece in that one, or the window pieces from my daughter's rooms and my studio; I see those as little shrines. I was thinking about faith and the idea of home, and why we feel attachment to a place. To me, it's more about the people, not necessarily the landscape, but the landscape is definitely going to play a part. That's also why the cookie-cutter houses make their way into the pieces, too. So again, yes, I think the layers and collage process are important because we have to think about the layers of history that create where we come from, who we are, where we're going. My daughter's window has all this random stuff that is collected but it's not completely meaningless. I'm sure there's something that I may have said to her, or her dad may have said, or maybe a friend that inspired her in some way. It shows how much these personal relationships impact where we've come from and where we go.

INTERVIEWER

Those pieces struck me in particular. It's interesting to hear you talk about them as little shrines or altarpieces, because they do feel like the collection of objects is very incidental overall. It's something that happened maybe with a little bit of intentionality, but mostly just because the objects have slowly come into the collection and had some significance—or maybe not. There's a range there, which itself resembles a slowly made collage but without the intention. In particular the refrigerator piece: that is totally a collage that was made over time on the surface of your fridge, but then ends up having a lot of meaning in that slow accumulation.

STONE-COLLINS

Right, yeah! You think about your everyday life, all the appointments that you have to keep and make and calendars, and, "Oh, I have to get my oil changed." We don't think of all that being important, but it all says a lot about us, like where we live, do we drive a car, do we have kids, what type of meetings are we going to, who's writing you a thank you note. You know other people keep journals, and for me this is just my way of documenting. I had to go back and find some images of some older work, some murals I did when we lived in Indiana and I was looking at some of the work that I'd done there and it *feels* like that period. It feels like that time in my life when I was figuring out who I am as a mom, as an artist, and trying to teach. These pieces feel like I figured a lot of that stuff out, but now I'm questioning my place in these spaces.

INTERVIEWER

So do you feel like you have some nostalgia for childhood? Or are there questions there about your own childhood?

STONE-COLLINS

Yeah, I think so, especially being raised in a pretty Evangelical background, and as someone who has constantly questioned that ever since I was old enough to question it. I have to think about all of that, because, to me, a lot of religion is about tradition and ritual and things that I crave in my life. But I feel like I have to become a lot more intentional about the traditions and rituals that I want to keep in my life and I feel like the work sometimes talks about that a little bit. Like in the refrigerator with the letters, you know, "I'm tired" or "FOMO" address what I'm just doing because it's expected versus what I really want to do. I think it's also questioning who we are as individuals and who we are in the collective. Within the roles that I have in my life as a mom, as a spouse, and a teacher, what do I really enjoy doing and what am I doing because I need to do it? Where do I really feel that I want to live and where do I just need to live at this time? How do those ideas intertwine?

INTERVIEWER

I see all of that in your work. I'm curious, though, how you come up with the finalized image. Do you have a bunch of objects that you are drawing and painting from and then arranging them in different settings, or is it more that you have a specific impetus for a piece where you want to recreate this thing and you do it through collage because it affords you a little more flexibility?

STONE-COLLINS

That's a really good question. All my pieces pretty much start with some type of sketch, and usually they are from photos. So the pieces in the neighborhood Over That Rainbow and Special Order 120, those were images where I was walking the dogs and maybe then there's a nice sunset. So I'm like "Oh, I'm going to take this picture." And so I started making these 5" x 7" paintings over the pandemic. I just refer to them as little studies, and it was mainly because I found coming into the studio and working on the collage work every day was too much. All of the work was becoming crap because I was like, "Oh, I've got this time. I've got to work in the studio." So every day when I wouldn't normally be in the studio I would just do those small little studies. A lot of the paintings start from that.

Pieces like the windows and the refrigerator, they'll start because I really will just find something that the kids have set up that's kind of ridiculous. Like the one that's my studio window, I just literally took a photo of it and that's pretty much everything that's there. I was just looking at the window one day and thinking about all the objects and how I have created this little shrine to myself but also to all these people who are in my life who have given me these different things.

And so then I started to think "Oh, I bet my kids do the same thing." So I took a picture of things in both of their rooms that are just kind of smushed together. It's the same thing with the refrigerator, and actually it's kind of funny…So we moved into the house that we live in now at the very end of 2020, and the refrigerator is not magnetic in this house. We had all this stuff that we brought from our old house and it was in a big tub, and I was just going to start putting the stuff back up on our new refrigerator, and then I realized it didn't stick. I kept the big tub that held all those magnets. And my daughter one day was like "I really miss having stuff on the refrigerator." So I thought, "I'm just going to make one." I literally just took out a lot of stuff from that tub and started painting it. Sometimes I do that when I get stuck. I just paint things around me, and so that's how a lot of the pieces start, too.

I think at the time I just didn't know what direction I wanted to turn next. The first thing I painted was the little note card guy that one of my daughters had made and it actually hangs up in my studio. One day I was like, "I'm just going to paint this and replicate it." And then I thought, "Why not just do that with a lot of their artwork and these, you know, 'get your tires rotated' reminders, and grocery list from 2 years ago that have all been in this tub forever?" I just think it was, again going back to this feeling of nostalgia, an, "Oh, I kinda miss this." Also, going back and looking at what was happening then, or remembering the kind of images my kids were drawing—you know those magnet letters, those are really something that my kids are too old for now, but a couple of years ago, my youngest would have been five. She would have really been using those a lot. So I think, again, this is just speaking of time and place and who we are and how we change and who makes us who we are. As mundane as that stuff is, I feel like no one really talks about living in the suburbs. That's not really discussed, but it's a big part of my life, so instead of shying away from it, sure, I'll paint my fridge and all these mom activities that I have to do. Yes!

INTERVIEWER

Totally! I'm always really suspicious of questions or conversations around an artist's identity as a woman or a mother when it isn't an intentional part of the work, but I really appreciate the authenticity of those elements in your work. I mean clearly you are a mom, even if I didn't know you, just looking at the work. It feels like you are tackling the idea of suburban mom-hood in a way that is very authentic to you, but is very relatable, too. It just isn't talked about in art very much, because so often the voices of women, particularly women dealing with these types of issues, haven't been as included.

STONE-COLLINS

There's a lot of great work out there that is about motherhood. But I kind of want to approach it differently. I love being a mom, but sometimes I am like, "Did I think about this?" Having kids, there was a period of my life for two years where I couldn't make anything because they were very small. I listened to this podcast with Amy Reidel, and it was right after we moved here and I was dealing with my husband's treatments for his illness, and my mom being sick, and I had a four-year old and a two-year old. And she was I think on *Studio Break* and she started talking about her mom going through cancer and she said something like "Yeah, I just didn't make any work and when I did start making work it sucked and it was horrible and it was crappy but I just did it." I was teaching at the time, and I was feeling like, well this is just it, I'm just going to teach and how can I really even do my work after not making anything. Then listening to that I was like, "No! I can make something and why do I have to make it for somebody else. I'm just going to document." That was my lightbulb of thinking, "Well, I'm not going to be ashamed of putting my artistic career on hold. I'm not going to be ashamed that I needed to move to the suburbs for family and health reasons." It was listening to her that gave me the permission to not make everything so beautiful or feel like it had to be about bigger issues. But these can also be big issues. These are issues that lots of people deal with, but nobody thinks that anybody else wants to know about them.

INTERVIEWER
I find it really refreshing, honestly. And Amy is so great.

STONE-COLLINS

Yeah, so it was her, and I've told her that repeatedly. You never know what you are going to say or write that gives people their own kind of lightbulb. For me it was like, "Oh yeah, of course– of course there is no rule book!"

Visual Art:
Alice Stone-Collins

Alice Stone-Collins, *Over That Rainbow*, Gouache on paper, cut and collaged, 48" x 30", 2021

Alice Stone-Collins, *Special Order 120* , Gouache on paper, cut and collaged, 48"x 30" , 2021

Alice Stone-Collins, *Objects in Mirror*, Gouache on paper, cut and collaged, 24″ x 30″, 2021

Alice Stone-Collins, *Roundabout*, Gouache on paper, cut and collaged, 20" x 24" , 2021

Alice Stone-Collins, *House of Smoke*
Gouache on paper, cut and collaged
20"x 24", 2021

Alice Stone-Collins, *Thermostat*, Gouache on paper, cut and collaged, 24″ x 30″, 2021

Alice Stone-Collins, *In the Garage*, Gouache on paper, cut and collaged, 24" x 30", 2021

Alice Stone-Collins, *The Invisible Hand*, Gouache on paper, cut and collaged, 32" x 20", 2021

Alice Stone-Collins, *@Home*
Flashe and Acrylic on Yupo
16′ x 5′ x 4′, 2021

Alice Stone-Collins, *Maintain an Even Temperature*
Gouache on paper, cut and collaged
30"x 64", 2022

Alice Stone-Collins, *Look Away*, Gouache on paper, cut and collaged, 24" x 30", 2022

Alice Stone-Collins, *Monday Afternoon*
Gouache on paper, cut and collaged
27"x 30", 2022

Alice Stone-Collins, *Sunday Morning*
Gouache on paper, cut and collaged
27"x 30", 2022

In Which My Father Cries Cicadas
by Jay Orlando

My father is clumsy with his tears
this is, presumably, due to a lack of practice
or perhaps a timidness
absent from his larger life

the drops leak out, slipping between his thick fingers
like a curse slips between lips
face veiled by his sandpaper hands
neck red as a pheasant's
a child's approximation of mourning

He drops these tears unpredictably
when he is drunk after too much rum
when *The Wreck of the Edmund Fitzgerald* plays
through the static of the pickup truck radio
after a long day at work
on the broken lawn mower, on the overgrown lawn
in the mid-July heat

They fall like porcelain
dolls in slow motion
tipping over and over in the air
and I am unable or unwilling
in my own clumsiness
to catch them
before they, as with cicadas swarming in the sun
become multitudinous
shattering, smearing, in beautiful sharp, soft ugliness
in a void of silence
whose white noise resonates
thick
in the quality of a bass note
up through the feet and onward
vibrating internally against my sternum
a feedback loop of quiet
growing in intensity
louder and louder
with every fumbled drop

Isolation Poem
by Victor Clevenger

sitting in a room alone
that suddenly seems as wide
as a night sky above an orchard's hills

i imagine death
holds an apple in his hand like a moon

smiles when nobody is looking   takes a bite

cracks fill full where lips meet like mighty rivers
that topple their banks running freely
beneath the bestubbled whiskers rooted
into a chin like a thousand stretched toes of trees
into dirt

off in the distance
i can hear the drowning tick
of every second pass

& i swallow

a heavy breath

Taking The Buick
by Henry Yukevich

My neighbor Bob was 93 when he passed away.
His son came by to pick up his stuff.
"We all gotta go some day" he said.
"Nothing is forever" he said. "Not even Bob."

Ninety-three divided by three is thirty-one.
"My wife, she works with these youths
These math whizzes.
Couple a brainiacs.
One time she took me to this competition for these youths
Quiz Bowls it's called or somethin'

"We drove all the way from Destin, Florida, ya know.
Over 30 one hundred miles.
The World's Luckiest Fishing Village, they call it."

"Anywho
The car in the garage
The Buick. Gold. LaCrosse. 2013.
Did you know it has 31 miles on it?
Dad only drove it to get donuts.
31 miles. Do you believe that?"

"In my life, I can remember three times I saw my father cry.
My sister, she was 31 when she passed.
Funniest thing about my sister,
When we were kids she used to always get the hiccups at church.
and me and Dad would start laughing so hard,
In church, ya know.
The kind of laugh where you're trying not to laugh."

"One of the things I learned from these youths, these math wizards is
All the things, all the, uh integers,
They all kinda fit together, ya know?"

"Anyways, I'm taking the Buick."

An Interview with Kimberly L. Becker

Of mixed descent, including Cherokee, Kimberly L. Becker is author of five poetry collections: *Words Facing East* and *The Dividings* (WordTech Editions), *The Bed Book* (Spuyten Duyvil), *Flight* (MadHat Press) and *Bringing Back the Fire* (Spuyten Duyvil). Her poems appear widely in journals and anthologies, including *Indigenous Message on Water*; *Women Write Resistance: Poets Resist Gender Violence*; and *Tending the Fire: Native Voices and Portraits*. Her work has been nominated for a Pushcart Prize. She has received grants from MD, NC, and NJ and held residencies at Hambidge, Weymouth, and Wildacres. Kimberly has read at venues from The National Museum of the American Indian (Washington, DC) and Split This Rock, to Wordfest. She has served as mentor for PEN America's Prison Writing and AWP's Writer to Writer programs. She currently lives in North Dakota but calls the mountains of North Carolina home. Her home on the internet is www.kimberlylbecker.com

The following conversation was conducted electronically over the Winter and Spring of 2021-22 and has been lightly edited for clarity.

Noah Soltau, Managing Editor

INTERVIEWER
The sacred and the natural are often intertwined in your work. How do you, as person and poet, uncover the sacred in the mundane?

BECKER
Mundane derives from "mundus," world. The world is sacred, its waters, all creatures, "all our relations," not just humans. Like everyone, I can get caught up in the stress of my job and to-do list and fail to notice occasions for gratitude in my life. North Dakota in the winter (when I first began responding to your interview questions) can be very harsh, with wind chills down to 40 and 50 below and white-out conditions, but there also sun dogs haloing the sun, snow sifting and shifting like sand across the highway, a gigantic white-for-winter jackrabbit running to elude a black dog. Even in killing cold that demands respect there is great beauty to be found.

Everything is sacred because Creator made it. It is humans who desecrate this world. It is the 7th hottest year on record and many people want to deny climate change? Theologian Matthew Fox has written about original blessing and creation spirituality (and I read Genesis in Hebrew in seminary and was struck by the repeated phrase, God saw that it was good), which is a bedrock of many Native traditions. Or as my Cherokee teacher explained it, when people danced around the fire, whites thought that "heathens" were worshipping the fire itself, when in reality they were worshiping the Creator who set the fire in the sky and in their hearts.

So I do not separate the sacred from the so-called mundane. Those of us of the Christian faith believe that Yeshua (a tribal member) became incarnate, enfleshed. Even if that story is only regarded as myth (and myth doesn't necessarily mean untrue), what could be messier, more mundane than taking on human skin and bone and sinew? As someone who has dealt with chronic pain for many years, I have often not wanted to be in my body. Since childhood, it has often been easier for me to dissociate, float away, imagine other worlds. My writing has simultaneously grounded me and helped me escape the physical world.

I do not separate my vocation as a poet from my vocation as a chaplain. I write out of the totality of my experience as a person who is only on this earth temporarily. Having witnessed many deaths as a hospice and hospital ICU and on-call trauma chaplain, I have come to see all life as sacred, including death, which a nurse of mine aptly called birth at the other side of the spectrum. It is sacred to watch someone take his/her/their last breath.

Read Joy Harjo's "Eagle Poem." It reads as a prayer. Rilke has this great poem basically asking how do you stand all the horrible things in life and the repeated answer is *weil ich rühme*, because I praise. So as a poet, I praise the broken beauty, but also take seriously the poet's responsibility to witness, which is why organizations like Split This Rock are so important. Poets and artists have a role to play in social justice. We create in response to what we see. Art can be powerful medicine, part of the healing, part of the call to action on behalf of this mundane and sacred world.

INTERVIEWER

Place figures heavily in many of your poems. Describe how being part of the Appalachian diaspora, so to speak, affects the way you think and write about it.

BECKER

Simon Ortiz has this great equation being + place = existence. This recognizes that we not from a place; we are *of* a place. I am a Southerner, born in Georgia, raised in North Carolina. I now live on the Northern Plains. I lived in Washington DC metro area for many years. I've lived in Germany, Maryland, New Jersey, Kentucky, Tennessee.

The mountains of North Carolina will always be home, but I've tried to make a home wherever I am, especially by trying to get to know the land, the water, the history of the Native peoples of the region. Although I am not enrolled as a member of a sovereign nation, I took to heart what my

Cherokee teacher said: that you can't be part Cherokee; you either are or you aren't, but if you say you are, he is going to expect something of you. So in my writing I try to honor my heritage. I carry home within me. Moving to and living in such a different environment from where I grew up has heightened this sense of an inner compass. Moving to such a strange (to me, as a Southerner) yet beautiful place of extremes here in North Dakota has inspired new work as I've tried to get to know this new land and appreciate the deep Native history here.

We're all in diaspora in some ways, and as someone with both Anglo and Native heritage I feel that I carry the colonizer within. Many of us also have immune issues, almost as if we are at war within ourselves. Paula Gunn Allen wrote about this in her poem describing her lupus: *a mixed breed woman can do nothing but fight*. I present white. I am accorded white privilege. People will say things to and around me assuming that is how I identity that they would not say if they knew I follow the Native path. A late friend of mine gave me life-changing advice years ago when he said I had to choose which path to follow, since white and Native cultural values are so different. I remain grateful to Sequoyah Guess for that wisdom. Diaspora, being scattered, is something many tribes were forced into. Jewish friends of mine are also in diaspora. Diaspora and the spore share the same root word. So might those of us in diaspora be spores that carry home wherever we are, including in our writing? I hope so. German has this great word, *Heimweh*, "home hurt," for homesickness. I have a poem of that title in my latest book. There's always that pull, that sense of pain at being away from home. Maybe writers seek to find our way home through our words and create new homes in our poems, especially when our home lives were hurtful.

INTERVIEWER

You have noted that the discovery of your Cherokee ancestry is a moment that serves as a site of both privilege and conflict. How does poetry in particular allow you to negotiate these different aspects of your identity?

BECKER

As part of my chaplain residency when I was an ICU chaplain, we studied intersectionality in the context of trauma-informed care. Each of us brings different identities to our work and personal lives. For instance, I am a cis gender female, formally educated, middle class, but whose mother was the first in her family to earn a college degree. In doing a genogram (also part of my residency) I could see the effects of intergenerational trauma and unresolved grief. Anyone of Native descent will carry intergenerational trauma within. For some, the cause is very evident from genocidal policies: being forced on the Trail of Tears or into government boarding schools. In my case, our Cherokee heritage is not documented, was kept secret, assimilation and hiding was the way to survive. Secrecy breeds shame. When I found out about my heritage, I was determined to break the silence and to do anything I could to try to reclaim and honor what little Cherokee blood I had.

In my professional life I have trained as a racial healing leader and was honored to use my facility with words to write a successful grant for environmental reparations for one of the tribes I work with. I do not presume to speak as a citizen of a sovereign nation. I try to listen and learn respectfully. One of the greatest honors of my life was being asked to adapt traditional Cherokee stories into radio plays, thanks to Shawn Crowe of EBCI (Eastern Band of Cherokee Indians), who had confidence in my ability to contribute. Poetry is where I go to sort through all the tensions and to try to find some measure of peace. I have an essay coming out in an anthology (*Unpapered*, University of Nebraska) of other undocumented writers. It's called "The White Box" and has to do with a hostile white cop who was mad I asked him to uncheck the white box and check mixed race instead when I got my driver's license in rural NC. I experienced fear that my darker-skinned friends experience on a daily basis. Coming to ND where there are overt tensions between Anglos and Natives has been eye-opening. I feel I have to walk both worlds and even code switch, while continuing to choose to follow the Native path. Someone at a work setting once patted me like a dog and said, "we love you *even though* you're part Cherokee."

INTERVIEWER

It's obvious that these moments of conflict deeply inform your poetic and professional lives. Resistance is a theme in your work, as are dreams; why do you think these liminal moments are so important?

BECKER

Dreams have always fascinated me. In the Bible, many messages come in dreams. As a kid, I dreamed vividly and with could even decide what to dream about. I left a job because of a dream. I was giving people a tour of my work place and said to them *it's beautiful, but you can't breathe*. I gave notice the next day. I was suffocating in that position. At the time, I was married and had the financial privilege to be able to do that. I do believe ancestors are always with us and often will visit or spirit walk through our dreams if we're paying attention. I do think artists of whatever genre are innately intuitive about observing our surroundings. For some of us, that stems from survival mode and the hypervigilance of PTSD. But being someone "on whom nothing is lost" (the novelist Henry James's description of a writer) also means we are sensitive to injustices and can witness to that in our work.

Several years ago I was protesting in Lafayette Square with other Split This Rock poets. There is power in gathered voices and in art. Why else do autocratic regimes want to silence artists? My first graduate degree was in German language and literature, back when there was still an East Germany. The state-imposed propaganda made for some terrible art, but there were those writers who found ways to resist and still retain artistic integrity. Artists can't be sycophants. My own work is nothing revolutionary. I just try to witness to events and encounters in my life that have moved me or pulled back the veil a bit on what the Celts would call thin places, since we're always, whether we recognize it or not, so close to the spiritual world.

Being attuned to those liminal moments can empower us to resist injustice. It is only when we see ourselves as part of a community needing compassion that we might offer our words in honor of those who might not be able to speak freely. But honestly, for me, writing is also a selfish act. It helps me purge what needs purging. A friend of mine asked me not too long ago, *how are you going to write now that you're happy?* That made me laugh, as it has tragic truth to it. All my life from childhood on I've written to survive. Now I write less for order and control and more to connect.

INTERVIEWER

The political, social, and cultural concerns in your work are evident, so what do you want poetry to do, and how would you describe the gap between what you want it to do, and what you see it doing?

BECKER

I guess I don't want poetry to do anything. Or rather, not set out to do anything. The beauty of the best poetry is that, by being, it is doing. Remember the story of Mary and Martha and Jesus saying Mary had chosen the better part not by doing but by being and listening? So maybe poets listen and then write what they've heard and in that writing, in that creating (poet means maker) a poem is now a testament to having listened. In my tradition, prayer is responding to God or Creator with or without words. And yet I begin each day facing East and offering prayers I was taught in Cherokee. So maybe my poems have been prayers all along. If my poems resonate with someone else then that is very gratifying. What was it Picasso said about all children are artists? All children are poets. It's only as we become adults that the world wants us to conform. Poets are then maybe the non-conformists, the resisters.

There's usually a very big gap between what I want my poetry to do and what I succeed in doing. Especially since having my brain surgeries (for trigeminal neuralgia) and now with brain fog from long covid, I'm often just not able to think of what Flaubert called "the right word." My vision of something rarely is executed to my satisfaction. I believe that poetry both grounds in us experience and helps us transcend it, especially the difficult times. When I was working at the hospital as an ICU chaplain, also taking call for level one trauma pages, I also would go in the hospital chapel and check the prayer requests. One was very raw, a prayer and accusation of lament: God, if you are real then fuck you for this. I was really intrigued by that, because clearly the petitioner believed in something larger than him/her/their self if only to rail against it. In the same way maybe poetry is just talking to ourselves, but in doing so reaching others as well.

INTERVIEWER

Relationships, ways of being with one another, are important to you, and you are embedded in networks of Native authors and artists. Whose work is most exciting to you right now, and why?

BECKER

I wouldn't describe myself as "embedded in networks;" however, I do have a few close writer friends with whom I keep up and whose judgment I rely on, namely Allison Hedge Coke, my literary elder and better, friend, and mentor, who taught me humility by her example. She told me that when we achieve something for ourselves then our responsibility is to hold the door open for others. I have been honored to serve as a mentor both for AWP's Writer to Writer and PEN America's prison writing programs. I am proud that my mentee, Deborah Jang, went on to publish her first book that was blurbed by Native literary giant, Linda Hogan. But I pretty much write in isolation.

There are poets whose work I return to again and again, but I try to keep up with what is going on. Anthologies like *New Poets of Native Nations* and *When the Light of the World was Subdued Our Songs Came Through* are exciting and important and the Inaugural Indigenous Nations Poets retreat in DC is also cause for celebration. We have had the first Indigenous poet laureate in Joy Harjo, a long-overdue recognition of those whose songs were first heard in this land. I got to shake her hand once, and even though I'm sure she doesn't remember it, it was an honor I still treasure to this day. Younger writers learn from the elders and new generations will have new takes on traditional stories. It is humbling to be even a small part of the conversation. As a child, my dream was to become a writer, and I am grateful for my vocation as a poet. It has saved my life more than once.

full moon and the sun shines
by Tohm Bakelas

new jersey is a frost bitten coffin
with miles and miles of pale clouds

every winter the birds disappear,
i'm left with crows that circle overhead

toward the end of january
sparrows and titmice return,
just in time to shake off suicide

at midnight, the flowers stop waving,
the dead pass through the living,
and i sit on my porch and scratch
at the black tarry sky with
broken glass just to
recall my name.

Eliza Jane in the Days After
by Barb McCullough

Dwarf strawberries bleed themselves to
embrace this black earth. Hands on your hips, you
conjure Sweet Annie with vetch, take sustenance
from his surrender, relief in Harry's pine gown...

Like a bowl, bottom emptied, belly
up and tin-spoon-scraped, you rise
a sunwise woman, with clabber and crock,
alive in the wet way white Sarvis blossoms drink...

In time, pitch pine limbs escape their
milky ends, breathe green buds in anticipation
of a starker noon. Ironweed shadows measure in deep
purple days, switch grass blades through the shadows
                                to scatter and creep.

Advice for Those Who Long to Go Barefoot in April
by Karen Weyant

This is what you already know: the world is still cold
and pavement and blacktop will freeze your soles.

But you may not realize how that first warm spell
leaves everything prickly: grass brittle and winter sharp,

old snow, blackened from car soot and gravel, has melted
into shards as sharp as glass. Even debris left behind

will leave marks: that cigarette butt's ashes will stain
your heels, an old plastic straw will slice your toes.

But especially dangerous is the spring rain that leaves
evenings coated in a fine mist that taunts you until

you pull off your boots and socks, the same rain that tugs
earthworms from their dirt homes to bask in warm puddles,

only to freeze, when the weather, always a tease,
suddenly goes cold, and you find yourself dodging

their bodies frozen in thin icy pools, reminding you
of what happens when anything turns without warning.

Begets Violence
by Mitch James

When my grandmother was dying, I watched my mother push pills into her mouth. She would slide a pill in, give grandma water, then slide another. She was precise with the placement, patient but methodical, her nails always done.

The guys pushed Black Cats in the mouths of the toads the same way. I saw them work harder at perfection than when trying to harm something. At first, I cried. I'd beg them to stop. Then, I thought I would pretend like I didn't care. Watch with ennui. But their actions never changed because what they did was never about me. It wasn't even about them. It was something much bigger than all of us, yet we were a part of it.

I took my part in it the following summer. I was taking out the trash and saw the first toad of the season, bounding through the belly of the patio light, and got an idea. A small creek meandered behind the house. Every spring it flooded the lot two properties down, making it a spawning ground. That night, after my mom left for work, I snuck out with an old shoe box. By the time my wet feet grew numb in the sinking cool of the spring evening, I held a box full of toads. It was hard to contain them. Some climbed over others, the bodies below springboards toward an exit. I carried the shoebox to the garage, an occasional thump against the lid. I put the box on the seat of the riding mower and went inside, so proud of myself I could hardly sleep.

My mom woke me for school when she got home, her head cocked and eyes squinted at how quickly I rose and moved about the room. I met her downstairs and ate Cheerios while she packed my lunch. We talked about what I'd be doing in school that day and about how she'd like to take Friday off so we could go to the zoo before it got too hot and crowded. School would be out soon, she noted, and the place would be swimming with people. I mostly grunted my way through the conversation. With my lunch packed, she reached over, took my empty bowl, and kissed me on the cheek. She wished me a good day and went to bed. I went through the garage on my way to the bus stop.

I should've stopped then, after the first failure. That was the sign that I was not the one to save something. But that's our greatest flaw and strength as I see it. We believe we can do anything and sometimes manage to, never mind that both success and failure often come at inordinate costs. But I didn't know that yet. The toads had simply escaped. That was all, the shoebox and lid on the floor. Light burrowed into the garage below the door where mice had chewed through the weather stripping. A small hole. A ray of light. All that's required to lose everything.

That night, I tried again, this time using a box to a kerosene heater mom hadn't repacked after winter. The heater box was tall so the toads couldn't hop out. After I'd been collecting them for two hours, the bottom of the box bowed like a belly, something I hadn't considered, so I dragged it into the garage. There were so many more in the box this time, yet they were calm. Occasionally, one would shift a leg or its body; otherwise, they laid still, aqueous eyes cast in all directions.

The next morning came quickly. Mom woke me, still in her work attire but jubilant because she'd gotten the following shift off so we could go to Family-Free day at the zoo. She expected me to be more excited, especially about missing school. When I didn't burst from bed, I could see her deflate a little. Her smile let go. She was tired too. I could see it, more tired than I'd ever been, and I wanted her to be happy and feel good, so I threw my blankets off and popped out of bed, and pretended to be happy, but she knew I didn't mean it.

I ate breakfast while she showered and dressed. We were both chirpy at the table, talking about what cool animals we'd see. Once her toast and coffee were gone, we were on the road. It was such a bright day, the sun more white than orange, and the air was warm enough to crack the windows. Once at the zoo, we parked and weaved our way through the exhibits on the asphalt walkways, steadily warming in the sun. We removed our jackets. Then I pulled the sleeves up on my shirt and wished I'd worn shorts instead of jeans. Instead of hot cocoa, like we'd discussed, we found ourselves eating ice cream from paper bowls because neither of us wanted to fight to keep it from melting down the cone. We were not the only ones surprised by the heat. Jewels of sweat spackled the blotchy skin of others at the zoo, sweat the shape of continents along their backs, dark stains below their arms. The animals in cages found shade, while the rest of us traipsed along and cast side glances at each other, pretending like we were not walloped by the sun we'd been waiting for since winter.

When the sun was past its zenith, my mom said it was time to go. We were both beat from walking and cooking in the first hot sun in eight months, so when we got back to the car, we climbed in and exhaled and just relaxed a moment, the smell of sun and sweat and warm damp hair filling the small space. Then my mother grinned. I asked her what. She asked if I wanted to go for a swim. I had no idea what she was talking about, but her mischievous smile made me laugh. I liked the game. I noticed when we left the parking lot, we went the wrong way. I looked at her and grinned and she grinned back, orneriness in her eyes. As we inched along the interstate, a giant resort emerged on the horizon, a resort that had a massive tube snaking in and out of it. A water slide. I looked at my mom, her face stone. I grinned. She asked, what? I looked away, the resort growing bigger and bigger. Then we took an exit and were there.

I swam the rest of that day and into the night, my lungs and eyes scorched from chlorine. Once in our room, my mom showered and changed and put on make-up. She painted her nails. By then I was fighting sleep, and she knew it. She tucked me in and petted my head and told me she was going downstairs for a drink, that I'd be locked in safe but that if I needed anything to call the bar. She wrote the extension on a hotel tablet and left it on the nightstand. I nodded and watched her do a couple more things before turning the lights down to leave. As she moved from the dark room and into the violent light of the hall, her body appeared to move through bright water. Then my eyes closed with sleep.

I woke from a dream.

I had been on a raft, floating down a meandering river but could hear the roar of water rushing in the distance. Ahead was a white line of tumult where the water pulled away from itself. I was alone on the boat and not frightened. The day was bright and the leaves green, the sun flensed to shards as they rustled in a breeze. The roar grew deafening, the world before me a hungry mouth.

Mom was asleep next to me, curled on her side, the blanket pulled to her chin. I got up to pee, and by the time I returned, mom was on her back, her finger sliding across her phone screen. When I crawled back into bed, she said we had to get a move on, old alcohol like pennies on her breath. Within the hour, we were in the lobby having continental breakfast. It was free, so I wanted to try everything. By the time I ate a Styrofoam bowl of every cereal, a waffle, eggs, bacon, sausage, and toast, a bear claw, oatmeal, yogurt and granola, I felt bloated and sick but proud that I had accomplished what I'd set out to do and at no cost to mom, never mind the looks. Mom had toast and coffee, and I asked her why she ate the same thing she eats at home when she could eat anything there for free, and she just smiled and touched my head on her way to refill her cup.

I slept most of the ride home but managed to wake once off the highway and onto the jerky roads of the neighborhoods. Tyler, one of the boys who I watched kill toads the summer before, was outside our house with his dog Pounce. They lay together in the yard, while Tyler searched through his phone. His bike was parked beside him. He had somehow finagled the hitch of the tow behind his dad used on his riding mower to the frame of the bike. In it were gallons of water lined like militia. Tyler jumped up when we pulled in, Pounce right behind him and chasing his own tail in excitement. Mom asked me what Tyler wanted, and I asked, how could I know? She said, lose the attitude.

We pulled into the garage and got out of the car. It was then I realized what I'd done. I held my breath and watched my mom, hoping she didn't smell it, but she did. She asked if I smelled that. I asked what? She said, that, and rounded the car, her face scowling more as she moved closer to the box. She leaned over it and inhaled, just to make certain, then glared at me. That was my chance to confess, but I didn't have the courage, so she pulled back the flaps. Tyler came to the garage, Pounce bounding around like he was on fire. Tyler asked what we were doing, then asked what the smell was, then asked mom what she was looking at, his voice like a ricocheted bullet in the small garage.

Mom looked at me. "What is this?" she asked.

I didn't respond.

"Are you going to be a serial killer? That's what this looks like, you know? What am I supposed to do about something like this?"

"I just wanted them to have to play a game where something didn't die," I said, my voice breaking.

Mom looked at me a long time. Just looked. "Get it cleaned up," she said, finally, turning from it all and going inside.

Once she was out of sight, Tyler burst towards the box. He jumped back dramatically, then stuffed his head in again. His mouth never stopped chirping about how crazy it was, how many there were, how they looked like balloons, how much they smelled, how they didn't have enough fireworks for that many, not in a million years. The whole time I dragged the box back to the burn pile, he just kept talking, and Pounce circled us, scrying the box, his wet tongue lulling across his sharp teeth. I laid the box on its side and lifted the end. The bodies slid down the cardboard in one great sound of static before tumbling like onside kicks into the fire ring. A miasma of corpses followed the bodies. Pounce circled us, jumping and barking. Tyler's mouth wouldn't stop moving. I puked, felt the forms of breakfast as they came up. Very little of the food looked as it did when it started, solids stewed to liquids, the frogs jagged, rigor mortis bodies in a pile of bloat.

I dragged the box back to the garage, Tyler and Pounce in tow. Tyler's words thrummed with the cadence of sprinter's feet, but I didn't hear anything he said. It was just tone. Once at the garage, the door was shut, and mom was somewhere inside, boxed up in the closed house. That's when I realized Tyler had stopped talking and was looking at me as if he had asked me a question, so I asked him, what? That's when he told me about the new thing with the chipmunks, where he'd go out to the cemetery and upturn a gallon of water into their holes until they came running out. Then Pounce would chase them down and kill them. Tyler was quite serious and somber as he explained. He peered at the tow-behind of gallon water jugs with a gentle finality. I pushed the box against the house. Nothing stirred behind the curtains. There were no sounds. I was not sure what to do next. I just remember that Tyler was silent and Pounce calm on our way to his bike.

[END]

A Little More
by Byron Hoot

The Little Winter with its frost holds on
obstinate in its grip refusing
release. Sometimes it's the small
things that will not let go –
a remembered kiss, a touch,
a word, a moment that felt
like it would never end.
I bow to the frost this morning.

First Bee of False Appalachian Spring
by Antonio Vallone

I open the front door
to bring in the mail. Unexpected
sunshine blinds me.

Blinking my sight back,
I hear buzzing.

A small bee slams against the storm door's
thermal glass not swapped out
for its screen yet.

The end of Pennsylvania's winter
is weeks away.

I could crush the bee
with this thick stack of junk mail
I'm holding.

I use it to brush the bee
into the temporary sunshine,

instead,
to let it take its chances,
like I will,

like we all will,
with the future's returning cold.

Contributors and Credits

Tohm Bakelas is a social worker in a psychiatric hospital. He was born in New Jersey, resides there, and will die there. His poems have appeared in numerous journals, zines, and online publications. He has published 18 chapbooks and 2 collections of poetry. His forthcoming collection, *The Ants Crawl In Circles* will be published by Whiskey City Press in Summer 2022. He runs Between Shadows Press.

Kimberly L. Becker is author of five poetry collections: *Words Facing East* and *The Dividings* (WordTech Editions), *The Bed Book* (Spuyten Duyvil), *Flight* (MadHat Press) and *Bringing Back the Fire* (Spuyten Duyvil). Her poems appear widely in journals and anthologies, including *Indigenous Message on Water*, *Women Write Resistance: Poets Resist Gender Violence*, and *Tending the Fire: Native Voices and Portraits*. Her work has been nominated for a Pushcart Prize. She has received grants from MD, NC, and NJ and held residencies at Hambidge, Weymouth, and Wildacres. She has served as mentor for PEN America's Prison Writing and AWP's Writer to Writer programs.

Ace Boggess is author of six books of poetry, most recently *Escape Envy* (Brick Road Poetry Press, 2021). His writing has appeared in *Michigan Quarterly Review*, *Notre Dame Review*, *Harvard Review*, and other journals. An ex-con, he lives in Charleston, West Virginia, where he writes and tries to stay out of trouble.

Victor Clevenger spends his days in a Madhouse and his nights writing. His work has appeared in print magazines and journals around the world. He is the author of several collections of poetry, including *A Finger in the Hornets' Nest* (Red Flag Poetry, 2018), *Corned Beef Hash By Candlelight* (Luchador Press, 2019), *A Wildflower In Blood* (Roaring Junior Press, 2020), *Scratching to Get By* (Between Shadows Press, 2021), and *47 Poems* (Crisis Chronicles Press, 2022). Together with American poet John Dorsey, they run *River Dog*.

John Dorsey lived for several years in Toledo, Ohio. He is the author of several collections of poetry, most recently *Your Daughter's Country* (Blue Horse Press, 2019), *Which Way to the River: Selected Poems 2016-2020* (OAC Books, 2020), *Afterlife Karaoke* (Crisis Chronicles Press, 2021), and *Sundown at the Redneck Carnival* (Spartan Press, 2022). His work has been nominated for the Pushcart Prize, Best of the Net, and Stanley Hanks Memorial Poetry Prize. He was the 2019 recipient of the Poetry Rendezvous' Terri Award.

Peter Faziani is the editor of *Red Flag Poetry*, a journal and small press that publishes poetry postcards. He has two collections of poetry; *Warning Shots* (2017) and *The City as Modern Mausoleum* (2019). From 2014-2017, he lived in Indiana, PA where he picked up more than just a few new phrases. He currently teaches at Michigan State University.

Kelly Hider is a regionally and nationally exhibiting studio artist living in Knoxville, Tennessee. She received her MFA from the University of Tennessee in 2011. Recent solo shows include exhibits at Unrequited Leisure in Nashville, and the Central Collective in Knoxville. Her work appeared on the cover of *Number: Inc.*, in 2016. She has been twice awarded Ann & Steve Bailey Opportunity Grants through the Arts & Culture Alliance's Heritage Fund in Knoxville and completed an artist residency at the Hambidge Center in Rabun Gap, Georgia in 2019. She now works at Arrowmont School of Arts and Crafts as their Youth Education Programs Manager, and facilitates ArtReach on the Road, which brings craft education to K-12 students throughout central Appalachia. Hider joined the Tennessee Craft Board in 2021.

Byron Hoot is a co-founder of The Tamarack Writers (1974) and The Fernwood Writers Retreat (2019) and author of *Piercing the Veil, The Art of Grilling, Monster in the Kingdom, Such Beautiful Sense, Poems From the Woods, In Our Time, These Need No Title,* and *Observations.*

Mitch James is a Professor of Composition and Literature at Lakeland Community College in Kirtland, OH and the Managing Editor at *Great Lakes Review.* You can find his latest fiction in *Made of Rust and Glass: Midwest literary Fiction Vol. 1, Flyover Country,* and *Flash Fiction Magazine,* poetry at *Peauxdunque Review* and *Southern Florida Poetry Journal,* and scholarship at *Journal of Creative Writing Studies.*

John C. Mannone's poetry appears widely, including *Still: The Journal*, *Mildred Haun Review*, *Bloodroot*, *Impressions Literary Journal* [and the 2020 Impressions of Appalachia Creative Arts Contest poetry winner], and *I Thought I Heard A Cardinal Sing: Ohio's Appalachian Voices* (ed. Kari Gunter-Seymour). He was awarded a Jean Ritchie Fellowship (2017) in Appalachian literature, and served as the celebrity judge for the National Federation of State Poetry Societies (2018). Recent poetry collections include *Flux Lines: The Intersection of Science, Love, and Poetry* (Linnet's Wings Press, 2021), *Sacred Flute* (Iris Press, 2022), and *Song of the Mountains* (Middle Creek Publications, 2023). He edits poetry for Abyss & Apex. A retired physicist, John lives in Knoxville, Tennessee.

Ashley Massey is a recent graduate of the Master of Arts in English Literature program at the University of North Alabama where she focused on Southern Gothic literature and Critical Prison Studies. She resides on a farm in rural Middle Tennessee where she is a small business owner (Flatwoods Fawn jewelry brand) and cattle caretaker. She is the founder of Law Co Cycle Sisterhood, which provides free menstrual products to people in her hometown. She currently teaches reading and writing courses through the University of North Alabama to students who are incarcerated.

Barb McCullough has divided her time over the last three decades between teaching and writing in both WV and OH. While a WV educator, Barb was active as a WV Humanities Scholar and member of the Blennerhassett Reading Series. In OH, Barb collaborated with the Ohio Valley Literary Group and Marietta College as editor, grants writer, and the Becky Thatcher Showboat readings coordinator. She later certified as an OSU Asian Studies Fellow. In 2018-2020, Barb performed with Women of Appalachia Speak. Her latest work is found in *I Thought I Heard a Cardinal Sing: Ohio's Appalachian Voices*, released in March 2020.

Jay Orlando is a trans, queer Appalachian from Western Pennsylvania. His family has lived in the same region for nearly 300 years, which is not nearly as interesting as it sounds. In his free time he enjoys fixing typewriters, practicing calligraphy, and watching the same documentaries 32 times.

Elaine Fowler Palencia, Champaign IL, grew up in Morehead KY and Cookeville TN. She is the author of two Appalachian short story collections, *Small Caucasian Woman* and *Brier Country*, and has completed a third collection that is seeking a publisher. She has also published four poetry chapbooks, a short monograph, *The Literary Heritage of Hindman Settlement School*, and a nonfiction book about her great-great grandfather from Appalachian Georgia, *"On Rising Ground": The Life and Civil War Letters of John M. Douthit, 52nd Georgia Volunteer Infantry Regiment* (Mercer University Press, 2021). She is the book review editor of *Pegasus*, journal of the Kentucky State Poetry Society.

Greg Ramkawsky currently calls Pennsylvania home where he lives with his wife and five kids. His hands are reliably dirty. Greg has been published by Red Flag Press, Vita Brevis Press, and his debut collection, *The Broom Tree*, is forthcoming by Unsolicited Press.

Alice Stone-Collins earned her MFA in studio art from the University of Tennessee and has exhibited her work regionally and nationally, and has been a resident artist at KMAC (Kentucky Museum of Art and Craft) and the David and Julia White Artist Colony in Ciudad Colon, Costa Rica. She has been featured on Studio Break and The Artists Mother Podcast and her work published as the cover art for *Aurora, The Allegory Ridge Poetry Anthology*. Alice is a faculty member at Georgia Gwinnett College in Metro Atlanta, where she invites others to explore and expose smaller and larger worlds of possibility.

Susan O'Dell Underwood is the author of *Genesis Road* (Madville 2022), and the forthcoming collection of poetry *Splinter*, about the Appalachian diaspora (Madville 2023). Her poems appear in a wide variety of anthologies and literary journals, including *Alaska Quarterly Review*, *Oxford American*, and *A Literary Field Guide to Southern Appalachia* (UGA Press). She has taught at Carson-Newman University since 1990.

Frank X Walker is a professor in the department of English and the African American and Africana Studies Program at the University of Kentucky and the founding editor of Pluck! The Journal of Affrilachian Arts & Culture. A Cave Canem Fellow and co-founder of the Affrilachian Poets, he is the author of eight collections of poetry including, *Turn Me Loose: The Unghosting of Medgar Evers*, winner of the 2014 NAACP Image Award for Outstanding Poetry; and *Buffalo Dance: The Journey of York*, winner of the Lillian Smith Book Award as well as two newer collections, *The Affrilachian Sonnets* and *About Flight*.

Karen J. Weyant is the author of two poetry chapbooks, and her poems and essays have appeared in the *Briar Cliff Review, Chautauqua, The Cumberland River Review, Crab Creek Review, Crab Orchard Review, Fourth River, Lake Effect, Rattle, River Styx*, and *Whiskey Island*. She lives, reads, and writes in northwestern Pennsylvania.

Henry Yukevich lives in Angola, Indiana. He enjoys science fiction movies and heavy metal music.

The editors would like to thank our contributors, donors, and the Carson-Newman Arts Initiative. This journal would not be possible without their generous efforts and support.

Made in United States
Orlando, FL
02 December 2024

54424054R00055